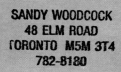

The Butterfly Night of Old Brown Bear

Nicolas van Pallandt

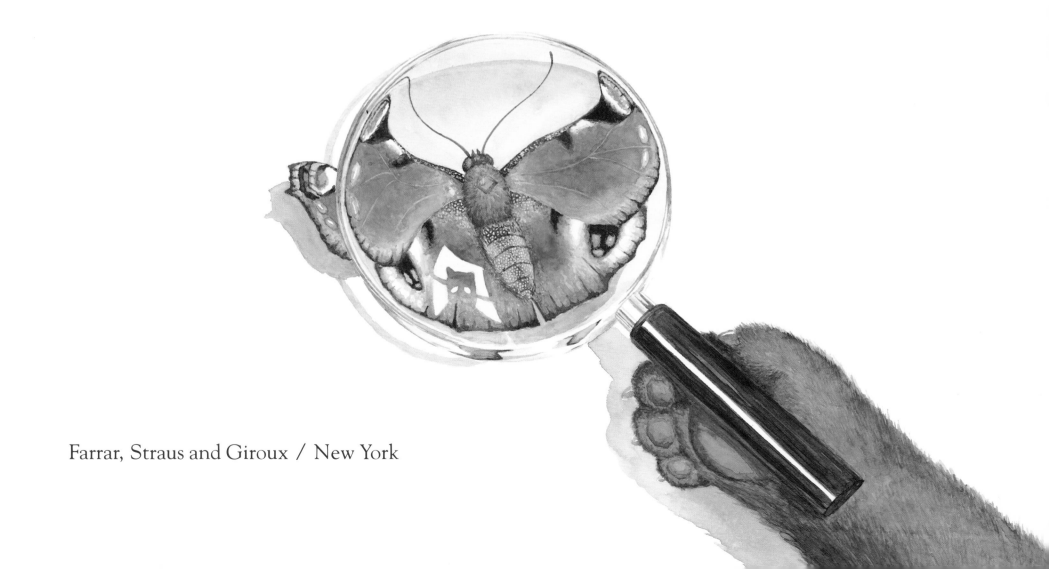

Farrar, Straus and Giroux / New York

Old Brown Bear collected butterflies and moths. Not just Long-Tailed Blues and Common Yellowbacks, but Pavonians and strange moths with names so long they stretched from his front door to the other side of the river.

One quiet evening, Old Bear was snoozing in
his garden when he felt a tickling on his toes.

He opened his eyes to see, perched on his big
toe, the brightest, most brilliant Blue Moth
that he had ever seen in his life. It waved its
hairy antennas at him and fluttered off into the
woods.

"Whillikers!" shouted Old Bear, leaping out
of his chair. He rushed into the house to fetch
his net. "A new, undiscovered species, and
it's *mine!*"

Away he went, with much whisking of his net.

Hare was sitting outside his front door when Old Bear whizzed by.

What's that old fuddy up to now? he wondered. "I say!" Hare called, bounding after Old Bear. "Hey, what are you doing?"

"Fiddle-faddle!" puffed Old Bear. "It's a *Discovernus bearus!*"

"A what?" said Hare. "What kind of name is that? Look, wouldn't you rather come back to my place and have a cup of tea and some lettuce?"

"My moth!" said Old Bear hotly. "I will name it! Off and away!" Then he muttered, "Young whippersnapper."

And Old Bear missed the Moth again. Up a stony hill it flew, with Old Bear swatting away behind it.

On top of the hill sat Old Man Elm, and up into his craggy branches flew the Moth.

"Old Man Elm," panted Old Bear, "I'm after a Moth."

"Oh," groaned Old Man Elm.

"Now, look," said Old Bear. "It is a new, unknown species!"

"Very well, very well. Climb up, then," grumbled the tree.

"Thank you," replied Old Bear, and swung himself up.

"Young whippersnapper!" muttered Old Man Elm, who was 243 years older than Old Bear.

Up and up Old Bear climbed until he stood perched on his toe on the teeniest, tiniest, topmost twig of the tree.

And still the Moth flew higher.

At that moment a small night cloud wafted by.

"Aha!" Old Bear cried, and, leaping up,
he clambered on board. The cloud was spongy
beneath his paws.

"This is fine," he cried in delight.

The Moth flittered by, and Old Bear hopped
along behind, feeling more spry by the minute.

"Good gracious," he said, giggling, "what a long way up it is. Hallo, Hare, down there, hallooo!"

Up the cotton-candy mountains he climbed until he stood on the uppermost point of the uppermost cloud.

And still the Moth flew higher.

"I am not giving up now!" shouted Old Bear.
So he hooked his net on the lowest mountain
on the moon and shinnied up.

Over the craters and deserts he ran with big,
bouncy moon steps. But Old Bear had forgotten
something very important: once a month the
moon disappears, which is exactly what was
happening at that very moment.

Soon there was only half a moon left, then even less. Suddenly Old Bear found himself standing on the last crescent of the vanishing moon.

And still the Moth flew higher.

Tired and angry, Old Bear made one final leap. Up went Old Bear. Up went the Moth. And down went Old Bear. Whoosh! through the clouds, and crunch! through the trees, onto the ground with a tremendous bump.

"Drat!" he said, picking himself up. He padded back into his house to look at his butterflies and moths.

But oh, how dull and how drab they looked, and how beautiful the bright Moth in his dream had been. Old Bear scratched his nose thoughtfully. Then he had a grand idea: he would set them all free. In bright daylight, he thought, they will be as gay and as beautiful as my dream Moth.

The butterflies and moths fluttered away, down the river and out of sight.

Old Bear was happily on his way home when Hare came rushing up.

"A moth!" he huffed. "Big, bright, blue, new, for you, over there!"

Old Bear frowned. "Piffle," he declared.

"Eh?" Hare's jaw dropped.

"Collecting is for bored people," Old Bear said, sniffing. "Take my advice, and do something with your life!"

"But..."

"Young whippersnapper," Bear grumbled. Then he stopped. After all, it *had* been fun, not the catching—he no longer cared if he caught anything—but the *chasing*.

Sheepishly he took his biggest net...

and the rising moon found Old Brown Bear
happily chasing bright butterflies across a field of
marshmallow clouds.